MIRRORS
OF THE
MIND

Unravelling The Truth

(A Series of Short Stories)

MIRRORS OF THE MIND

Unravelling The Truth

(A Series of Short Stories)

PREMACHANDRAN M.K

Clever Fox®
PUBLISHING

Chennai • Bangalore

CLEVER FOX PUBLISHING
Chennai, India

Published by CLEVER FOX PUBLISHING 2025

ISBN: 978-93-6707-258-5

Contents

Prologue

"There are no facts, only interpretations."

– Friedrich Nietzsche

Acknowedgement

A heartfelt shout out to my mentor, Sumedha Bhaduri, for encouraging me and supporting me in turning the story in my mind into a book. I am also deeply grateful to my family and friends for their constant motivation and help with proofreading; this book would not have been possible without them.

MY PERSPECTIVE
JUNE 15, 2010

Red in the Rain

At around 10:30 p.m., my final meeting of the day wrapped up. I let out a long, tired breath, feeling the weight of the past week loosen its grip, if only a little. It hadn't just been tough on me; my entire team was drained. Weekends had blurred into workdays, and the constant pressure had finally pushed me into the hospital with high blood pressure just a week ago.

Now, with our final delivery completed, we could finally pause, at least for a couple of days. I slung my laptop bag over my shoulder and headed down to the basement parking, the quiet hum of the office corridors behind me.

As I walked, one thought kept pushing its way through the fog in my mind: Priya. For six months, work had swallowed every moment, and she had grown increasingly worried about my health and the endless hours this new project demanded. I knew she was right. I had promised her and myself that once this was over, I would take a break, step away from the grind, and take her on that vacation we kept talking about.

I dialed Priya as soon as I got into my car. She picked up the second ring. Her voice coming through the Bluetooth speaker made me more relaxed and happier.

"I am on my way Priya, and will be there in an hour," I said.

"Wow! That is a surprise, Sid! I thought today you would start after midnight. Be careful, it is raining cats and dogs, so drive carefully. By the way, I have made fish Biryani for dinner," said Priya.

Fish is always my favorite dish and Priya knows that very well.

"Cool! I cannot wait. See you in a jiffy. Bye," with that, I kept the phone and drove out of the parking lot.

As I joined the traffic, the windshield was suddenly bombarded by sheets of rain. I hadn't realized how heavy it was while inside the office.

I turned on the defogger and the wipers and focused on the road ahead.

Our house was on the outskirts of Bangalore; Priya's idea. The city had become too congested, too loud. We'd found a peaceful villa community a good drive away. It cost more than we could afford, but it was safe and quiet, and our close friends, Shyam and his family, lived there too. Shyam, a college buddy, was now a sub-inspector at the local station. We'd been through a lot together. He was like a brother, dependable, loyal. The kind of friend who would show up at 3 a.m. without asking why.

His daughter, too, was a bright light in our lives, especially after we discovered Priya couldn't have children. The little one had grown into a bridge between both our homes.

The rain grew heavier, turning city roads into puddled chaos. Around 11 p.m., I finally broke free from the congestion and hit the national highway. The road stretched ahead, empty and dark, just the kind of drive I usually enjoyed. But not tonight.

Tonight, something felt...off.

The rain blurred the road markings. I squinted through the glass. Fatigue tugged at my senses. That's when my phone rang again; Priya, probably checking in.

I glanced at the screen for just a second.

"THUD!"

A sharp jolt. A deafening sound. I slammed the brakes. The car screeched and skidded before coming to a dead stop.

The phone kept ringing.

My hands trembled as I cut the call. My heart pounded so loudly it drowned out the storm.

Did I just hit someone?

I forced the gear into park and stepped out into the rain. It hit me like a wall. Headlights barely cut through the downpour. But then — I saw it.

A body. Lying face down on the side of the road. A pool of red streaming outwards, mixing with the rainwater.

He was wearing a white T-shirt and blue jeans. Young. Motionless.

My stomach twisted. I took a hesitant step closer. His head had taken the hit. There were no signs of life.

Panic surged. No witnesses. No one in sight.

What do I do? What if he's dead? What if this ruins everything, my career, my life, Priya...?

My thoughts spiraled. I stood frozen for a few seconds. Then I turned and ran back to the car, slammed the door shut, and drove off, leaving the scene behind.

The Man Who Wasn't There

I reached home close to 2 a.m.

Priya opened the door, her face instantly contorted in worry.

"You're soaked! What happened, Sid? Are you okay?" she asked, trying to dry me off with a towel.

I didn't answer. I walked straight to the bathroom and turned on the shower. Hot water poured over me, but it couldn't wash away the image of that body. That blood. That T-shirt. That rain.

Priya knocked on the door, her voice frantic. "Sid, talk to me! You're scaring me!"

"I'm okay. Just had a small accident," I replied. My voice cracked.

When I finally stepped out, Priya was waiting with a glass of water. Her eyes widened.

"Sid... I checked the car. The front is badly damaged. That's not a small accident. What really happened?"

I couldn't hold it in anymore.

"I think... I think I killed someone."

Her breath caught.

"What?!"

"I didn't mean to. It was raining heavily... and he just... appeared. I hit him, and I panicked. I didn't know what to do. I ran, Priya. I left him there. I didn't even check if he was alive."

For a moment, she said nothing. Then she took my hands in hers.

"Sid, listen to me. Let's call Shyam. Right now."

I nodded. She picked up the phone.

"Shyam, Priya here. Sorry to call so late. Sid's home and okay, but he hit someone on the highway. He thinks it could've been serious."

"Okay. Tell him not to talk to anyone," Shyam replied. "I'm out on election duty, but tell Sid to send me the exact location. I'll have the patrol check it out."

I took the phone. "It was at the T-junction near the temple. Just before the turn into the service lane."

"Got it. Don't worry. I'll update you as soon as I hear from them."

The next twenty minutes crawled like hours. I sat next to Priya, my fingers clenched tightly. I kept replaying the moment in my head. The clothes. The blood. The stillness. That couldn't have been a mistake.

The phone finally rang. I put it on speaker.

"Sid, my man. The team's checked the whole stretch. There's no body. No man. Just a dead dog… white-furred, hit hard, lying in a pool of blood."

I blinked. "What?"

"Yeah," Shyam chuckled softly. "Probably a street dog crossing the road. That's all there is. No sign of a person."

"No, Shyam... I saw him. A young man. White T-shirt. Blue jeans. He was right there."

Shyam paused, then said, "Buddy, you've been pushing yourself too hard. Maybe your mind played a trick on you. The dog's blood, the rain... you thought you saw something else."

I couldn't believe it. My heart had been convinced. My guilt had been real.

Priya placed a hand on my shoulder. "Sid, you need to rest. You've been burning out for months. Maybe it wasn't what you thought."

Maybe.

But as I lay in bed, drifting into a restless sleep, the image returned: the white shirt, the blood, the silent figure crumpled on the roadside.

PRIYA'S PERSPECTIVE JUNE 15, 2010

The Hallucinations

Lately, Priya had grown increasingly worried about Sid. His job had always demanded long hours and high stakes, but the past few months had pushed him to a breaking point. Deadlines piled on like collapsing dominoes. His phone never stopped buzzing; calls at midnight, emails before sunrise.

At first, she brushed it off. It was just another busy cycle, she told herself. But then Sid began to say strange things. He casually mentioned hearing footsteps echoing through empty office corridors, or seeing fleeting shadows that vanished when he turned. He laughed it off, blaming sleep deprivation or "too much caffeine."

But Priya wasn't laughing.

For the past few weeks, she'd been researching stress-induced hallucinations. What she discovered unsettled her deeply, it was far more common than people assumed, especially in high-performing individuals who refused to rest. Chronic anxiety, overwork, and severe sleep loss could trigger both visual and auditory hallucinations. The worst part was, Sid refused to believe anything was wrong.

The incident that truly shook her happened just last Sunday.

They had gone out for dinner, a rare break in their chaotic routine. The roads were empty on the way back, and the car moved smoothly through the late-night silence. Then, without warning, Sid slammed the brakes.

Priya's body jerked forward, her heart racing. "What happened, Sid? Are you okay?" she asked, alarmed.

He pointed straight ahead. "Didn't you see? Someone just crossed the road!"

But there was no one. The street was deserted. Just rain-slicked asphalt and flickering streetlights.

Priya's stomach dropped.

She knew instantly: Sid had imagined it. And the frightening part was, he didn't realize it.

Now, tonight, things had spiraled even further. Sid had come home drenched, shaken, claiming he'd hit a man on the highway, described the blood, the clothes, even the silence.

But when Shyam's team went to check, all they found was a dead dog.

Sid was convinced it was a man. He had seen it. Described it. Sworn by it.

Priya stood in the hallway, watching him try to sleep, his face restless even in unconsciousness. She felt her chest tighten.

This had gone too far.

She knew she couldn't handle this alone anymore. It was time to get help, from family, from Shyam, from anyone who could guide Sid back to reality.

Whatever it took, she would do it.

She wouldn't lose him to the shadows.

Light After the Rain

My disturbed sleep was interrupted by the alarm at 6 a.m. Sunlight streamed through the curtains, a bit too bright for comfort. In the distance, I heard soft clattering; Priya was already in the kitchen.

Moments later, she entered the room with a cup of steaming tea in her hand.

"Sid, today you're not going anywhere," she said gently, placing the cup on the bedside table.

She sat down beside me. "We're meeting Uncle Rajeev at 11. Please don't say no this time."

Dr. Rajeev — her maternal uncle — was a well-known psychiatrist at NiMS Hospital. Priya had mentioned seeing him before, but I'd always brushed it aside, convincing myself I just needed more rest or fewer deadlines.

I looked at her. "Do you really think it's necessary?"

"Very much," she replied without hesitation. "You've been under too much stress for too long. Something has to change, Sid."

Her voice was calm, but her eyes held worry. And she wasn't wrong. Maybe the pressure really *had* started to affect me. The visions, the fear, the accident, or whatever it was, it had all begun to feel like a blur. Had I really imagined it? Was I hallucinating? Could it be something worse? Schizophrenia?

I didn't share those thoughts aloud. No point in making Priya more anxious than she already was.

At around 9 a.m., Shyam and Meghana dropped by. Shyam, in full uniform, looked like he was on his way to work but couldn't resist a quick visit.

"Sid! Hope you slept like a baby," he grinned. "Still can't get over the fact that you imagined a dog in a T-shirt and jeans!" He burst into his signature loud laugh.

Priya frowned, but Meghana jumped in before she could respond.

"Shyam, please. This isn't the time for your stupid police jokes."

"Okay, okay. I'm done," he said, still chuckling. "Anyway, I owe you a drink tonight for saving you from this 'dog case'. What time should we meet?"

I glanced at Priya. "How about 9? A relaxed dinner. What do you think?"

Priya smiled. "Absolutely. Let's do that. And bring Aarushi along, I miss her."

Aarushi, their daughter, was home for Diwali break from her MBBS course in Delhi. She was like a ray of sunshine whenever she was around.

By the time we reached NiMS hospital, it was nearly 11:30. Dr. Rajeev greeted us in his usual warm and grounded manner.

"How are you two?" he said, ushering us in.

After some small talk, he asked Priya to wait outside so he could speak with me privately.

In the calm, neutral space of his office, I found it easier to talk. He listened carefully as I recounted what had been happening, the stress, the fatigue, the incident on the highway. In return, he shared stories of others who'd experienced similar hallucinations triggered by extreme burnout. He explained it as a form of "waking dreams" — the brain trying to process too much without rest, sometimes blurring the lines between reality and illusion.

By the end of the session, he handed me a prescription for mild anti-anxiety medication and insisted I take a month-long medical break.

The first thing I did when I got home was call the office and inform them I'd be going on medical leave.

That evening, we gathered at our home for dinner. Shyam and Meghana arrived with Aarushi, who brought along her guitar. The aroma of Priya's cooking filled the house; biryani, fried fish, and warm phulkas. For the first time in weeks, I felt like myself again.

Laughter bounced off the walls. The strains of Aarushi's music added a gentle rhythm to the evening. I looked around, at the food, at my friends, at my wife, and felt a quiet sense of gratitude. I was lucky. Not everyone gets a second chance to slow down.

Over the next few weeks, I began regular sessions with Dr. Rajeev. Gradually, I opened up more. He helped me recognize the negative thought patterns I'd been stuck in, the perfectionism, the pressure, the self-doubt. I learned techniques to manage my stress: deep breathing, mindfulness, structured breaks. I understood the importance of boundaries, of saying *no* when necessary, and asking for help when needed.

Therapy gave me tools, but more importantly, it gave me perspective. Seeking help wasn't a sign of weakness. It was an act of courage. Accepting that I needed support allowed me to start healing.

Meanwhile, life outside our home was anything but calm.

Our township was abuzz with police activity. A 25-year-old man, the son of a prominent politician, had gone missing. The word on the street was that it could be a kidnapping. Shyam had been assigned the case and was knee-deep in the investigation, often working late hours.

Despite the chaos outside, our home became a sanctuary. Priya was happier too, more at peace seeing me slow down, sleep better, smile more.

By the end of the month, I returned to work. But I wasn't the same.

This time, I carried with me a quiet determination, that no project, no deadline, no ambition would ever cost me my mental peace again. Work-life balance wasn't just a buzzword anymore. It was my lifeline.

APRIL 10, 2023

The Get Together

Shyam and Meghana were back in our township after nearly a decade. A lot had changed in those ten years, but some bonds, like ours, had only grown stronger.

Shyam had played a pivotal role in solving the mysterious disappearance of the MLA's son. The boy, under the influence of alcohol, had driven off the main road and plunged into a deep gorge near the forest reserve. It was Shyam's relentless investigation that helped crack the case. As a result, he was promoted to Assistant Commissioner and posted to Karwar.

Now, after ten long years, he had finally secured a posting back in Bangalore.

I was genuinely excited. I had missed having him around. No number of phone calls could match the joy of catching up in person.

"Priya, please hurry! We're going to be late," I called out, rushing down the stairs.

That evening was extra special, Aarushi was also flying in from the U.S. for a short break. Shyam and Meghana had arranged a family get-together to celebrate.

While Priya was still getting ready, I found myself pausing for a moment. Time had flown. Aarushi was no longer the curious teenager we knew, she was now a practicing doctor in the U.S., having completed her MBBS and MD.

"Sid, don't forget the cake!" Priya reminded me as she came down the stairs. Even after two decades of marriage, she looked stunning, grace etched with years of love, laughter, and resilience.

We reached Shyam's place around 6 PM.

"Finally, the lovely couple arrives," Shyam beamed as he opened the door, his warm smile unchanged.

He looked every bit the senior officer now, yet in this moment, he was just my old friend, excited for an evening off duty.

It was a beautiful day, a clear blue sky overhead, and the soft warmth of early summer in the air.

"Oh Priya, you look stunning in that chiffon saree!" Meghana said as she brought out marinated kebabs to the barbeque stand.

"We've all been so busy lately, man. Missed your company," Shyam said while lighting the barbeque.

"Where's Aarushi?" I asked, glancing around.

"She went out to get some ice cream," Meghana replied, smiling.

As Priya and Meghana headed into the kitchen, Shyam handed me a chilled Kingfisher. "Cheers, man."

Soon the doorbell rang. Aarushi walked in with her usual spark.

"Hey Aarushi! How are you doing?" I was thrilled to see her.

"All good, Uncle. It's been such a long time! How are you and Aunty?" she asked, giving me a warm hug.

"Look who brought your favorite banana cake," Priya said, appearing from the kitchen.

"Ah! I missed you both, and these yummy banana cakes!" Aarushi said, biting into a slice with delight.

The rest of the evening was filled with laughter, food, and stories, mostly Aarushi's funny and insightful tales from her time in the U.S. Her energy lit up the house.

Later that night, Shyam and I sat in the balcony, a bottle of Jack Daniel's between us, while the women busied themselves with dinner.

The breeze was soft; the night hinted at the arrival of summer.

Shyam poured me a drink. "Sid, tell me something honestly, did you ever have any more hallucinations after that… incident?"

"Fortunately, no," I said, taking a sip.

"To be honest, Shyam, I don't think I ever thanked you enough. If you hadn't found the truth, I'd have spent my whole life burdened with guilt."

"That's what friends are for, Sid. Cheers to that, all's well that ends well." He raised his glass.

We clinked glasses. A quiet toast to closure.

"You know what?" I chuckled. "After that incident, I installed a dashcam in my car. Just to be sure I wasn't imagining things anymore!"

"That's brilliant!" Shyam burst into laughter. "Priya's idea?"

"Of course!" I grinned. "She always has the best ones."

And we laughed like old times, grateful for the moments, the memories, and the friendships that had stood the test of time.

Some Truths Remain Unspoken

As the party ended, Meghana and Aarushi busied themselves with the dishes, while Shyam slipped away to his room for a quiet drink. He stood by the French windows, sipping slowly, lost in thought, when Aarushi entered silently and closed the door behind her.

"Dad, we've never really talked about that night," she said gently. "Don't you think Sid uncle deserves to know the truth?"

Shyam didn't turn around. His eyes stayed fixed on the darkening skyline. "No, Aarushi. Some truths, if revealed, only reopen wounds. If a lie brings peace, let it remain."

"But you've carried this alone for so long. Doesn't it weigh you down?" she asked, her voice cracking just a little.

He finally turned, a faint smile on his lips. "I'm not in pain, beta. I have you, safe, happy, standing beside me. I have Sid, just a few blocks away, alive and doing well. That's more than enough for me."

He paused, then added, "The only regret I carry is not being able to thank Sid for what he unknowingly did for us."

Aarushi reached out and hugged her father tightly. "You've always taught me to do what's right. I just wish we hadn't needed to lie to do it."

"You did the right thing, Aarushi. And you must never feel guilty for protecting yourself. You were brave, and I'm proud of you."

She left the room quietly, leaving Shyam alone with his thoughts.

He poured another drink, his hand trembling slightly. The image of that night, the screech of tires, the crash, the panic, still haunted him. What if Sid's accident hadn't happened? What if that moment hadn't changed everything?

The questions lingered like smoke in the room, but the answer, as always, stayed locked away in his heart.

AARUSHI AND SHYAM' S PERSPECTIVE JUNE 15, 2010

Rain, Silence, and a Lie

The music at the alumni party thudded through the air, loud enough to make conversation nearly impossible. Aarushi stepped away from the dance floor, hoping for a quieter corner, when Sanjana approached her.

"Aarushi, Neha had to leave early, her mom's unwell. She asked me to let you know," Sanjana said.

Panic pricked at Aarushi's chest. It was almost 10 p.m. She had only been allowed to attend on the condition that she and Neha would return home together. Now, she'd have to find another way back.

Calling a cab was out of the question, her mother had strictly forbidden solo rides at night. Her eyes swept across the crowd for a familiar face, and that's when she spotted Vicky near the bar counter, surrounded by friends.

He stayed in the same township as her. Though they'd exchanged polite hellos during community events, they had never spoken much. Still, in that moment, he was her best option.

She hesitated but walked over. "Hi Vicky, would it be alright if you dropped me home? Neha had to leave early."

"Sure! I was thinking of leaving around 10:30. Let's go then," he replied with an easy smile, before turning back to his friends.

By the time the party wound down, rain had begun to fall, a light drizzle at first, then a heavy, rhythmic downpour. Aarushi waited outside the restaurant, shivering slightly. Vicky pulled up with his car and rolled down the window.

"Let's go!" he called out.

She got in, taking the passenger seat. Water streaked down the windshield as they started driving through the quiet roads.

"Vicky, I hope you haven't had too much to drink," she said cautiously.

"Just two pegs of vodka. I'm good," he grinned.

But it didn't take long for her discomfort to grow. Vicky's tone shifted, his speech slurred slightly, and he veered into stories about his escapades with women. Aarushi stared ahead, wishing the road would speed up.

She debated calling her father. But the thought of disturbing him at work, or worse, making him worry, held her back.

Suddenly, she froze. Vicky had placed his hand on her thigh.

"Don't," she snapped, shoving it away and shifting closer to the door.

"Relax, Aarushi. I didn't mean to scare you," he said, laughing under his breath.

Her pulse pounded. It was now 11:30 p.m., and they were driving on a deserted stretch of highway. She fumbled for her phone and began typing a message to her dad. Sensing her fear,

Vicky suddenly swerved off the highway into a narrow, unlit lane.

"What are you doing?" she cried. "Stop the car. Right now!"

Vicky turned off the engine, hit the central lock, and leaned toward her. "You've been on my mind for a long time. Ever since I saw you at the township events... I just wanted a chance to get close."

He tried to grab her.

Aarushi fought back, a sharp kick to his stomach gave her just enough time to unlock the door and scramble out. Rain lashed at her face as she bolted across the road into the thick forest brush lining the highway.

Behind her, she heard him yell, "You can't run from me, bitch!"

She crouched low behind a bush, barely breathing, her phone in her hand. She was about to call her dad, but the screen's glow might give her away. She hesitated.

Then — headlights. A car tore down the highway. Vicky, scanning the brush, spotted a glimmer of light and stepped into the road.

"Thud!"

The sound was sickening. Aarushi peeked through the rain. Vicky lay motionless. The driver stepped out, and in the flash of the headlights, she saw him.

Siddharth Uncle.

He stood frozen for a second, then turned and got back into the car. The taillights disappeared into the rain.

Aarushi stared at Vicky's body, soaked and still. Her entire body trembled. After a moment, she found the strength to unlock her phone and dial the one number that made her feel safe.

"Papa," she whispered, when he answered.

And then she broke down.

The Weight of Silence

It was around midnight when Shyam's phone rang. Seeing Aarushi's name flash on the screen, he assumed she was calling to say she had reached home after her alumni get-together.

"Hi Aarushi…" he began, but before he could finish, he heard her wailing on the other end.

"Aarushi? What happened? Are you okay?"

"Dad… can you please come pick me up? I'm in real trouble."

His heart skipped a beat. Shyam rushed out of the police station, jumped into his jeep, and started the engine.

"Send me your location. I'll be there in fifteen minutes," he said, trying to mask the rising panic in his voice.

The rain outside was relentless. He knew that stretch of the national highway well; isolated, dark, and desolate at this hour. Not a place for his daughter to be stranded.

As he neared the location, headlights revealed Aarushi standing drenched on the side of the road. Her body trembled, whether from cold, fear, or shock, he couldn't tell. He pulled over immediately.

The horror of the situation hit him when she led him to the spot. There, on the muddy side-lane, lay the lifeless body of Vicky, son of MLA Nageswara Rao. Aarushi, sobbing, recounted everything in fragments: the attempted assault, her desperate escape, and the moment of impact, Vicky being run over by a car in the rain. She had seen the driver. It was Sid.

Shyam's blood froze.

"Go sit in the jeep, Aarushi. Lock the doors. I'll handle this."

He bent down to check Vicky's pulse. Nothing. Dead.

Shyam looked around. Just across the road, a stray dog lay crushed under another vehicle. An idea sparked. The stakes were too high. The name involved too powerful.

With grim resolve, he pulled on his gloves, dragged the dog's carcass to Vicky's side, and then carefully lifted Vicky's body into the boot of his own car.

He drove Aarushi home first. "You can't tell anyone about this. Not your mom. Not even Sid. Do you understand?" She nodded tearfully.

After dropping her off, he didn't stop to go inside. He turned back, driving into the storm.

Vicky's car was still where it had been. As he contemplated his next move, his phone rang again. It was Priya.

"Shyam, Sid met with an accident," she said in a trembling voice.

"Okay. Tell him not to talk to anyone," Shyam replied.

"Shyam, Priya here. Sorry to call so late. Sid's home and okay, but he hit someone on the highway. He thinks it could've been serious."

But first, he had to finish what he had started.

He found Vicky's keys still in the ignition. Moving quickly, he hid his jeep behind the shrubs and drove Vicky's car to the forest road near Nandi Hills. Deserted. Silent. Perfect.

He shifted Vicky's body into the driver's seat. Then, after disengaging the parking brake, he watched as the car slowly rolled forward, gathering speed, until it plunged nose-first into the deep valley below.

He exhaled, but it didn't bring relief. It never would.

Picking up his phone, he called Priya. He had a plan now. He just hoped it would be enough to save everyone.

…IN THE SHADOWS

Back in the silence of his room, glass in hand, Shyam stared out the French windows as the rain softened into a drizzle. The storm outside had passed, but not the one within him.

He had carried the truth like a stone in his heart for years, its weight never lessened, only buried deeper with time. Aarushi's safety had come at a price. Sid's suffering, though unintentional, was part of that price. That was the truth he couldn't bear to share. Not then. Not now.

As he replayed Aarushi's visit to the room moments ago, he felt a strange relief. She knew. And yet, she stood beside him, without judgment, without blame.

That was enough.

Outside, the sound of laughter drifted in from the kitchen, Meghna and Aarushi finishing up. Life, as fragile and complicated as it was, had moved on. Shyam took a sip of his drink.

"Some truths," he murmured to himself, "are better left in the shadows... where they protect the ones we love."

And with that, he closed the curtain… feeling the silence of the night.

To Be Continued ...